The Riverboat Crew

OXFORD UNIVERSITY PRESS

OXFORD LONDON GLASGOW
NEW YORK TORONTO MELBOURNE WELLINGTON
NAIROBI DAR ES SALAAM CAPE TOWN
KUALA LUMPUR SINGAPORE JAKARTA HONG KONG TOKYO
DELHI BOMBAY CALCUTTA MADRAS KARACHI

© Andrew & Janet McLean 1978

First published 1978

Reprinted 1979

NATIONAL LIBRARY OF AUSTRALIA CATALOGUING IN PUBLICATION DATA

McLean, Andrew, 1946–
The riverboat crew.

For children.
ISBN 0 19 550571 9

1. McLean, Janet, 1946–   , joint author.
II. Title.

A823'.3

Typeset in 20Pt. Plantin by Savage & Co. Pty Ltd
Printed in Hong Kong by Liang Yu Printing Co.

Published by Oxford University Press,
7 Bowen Crescent, Melbourne

The Riverboat Crew

Andrew and Janet McLean

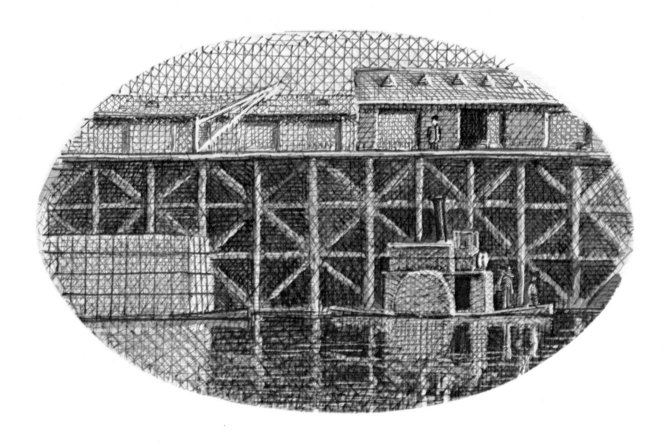

Melbourne
OXFORD UNIVERSITY PRESS
Oxford Wellington New York

The *Alice* was a paddle steamer
on the Murray River.

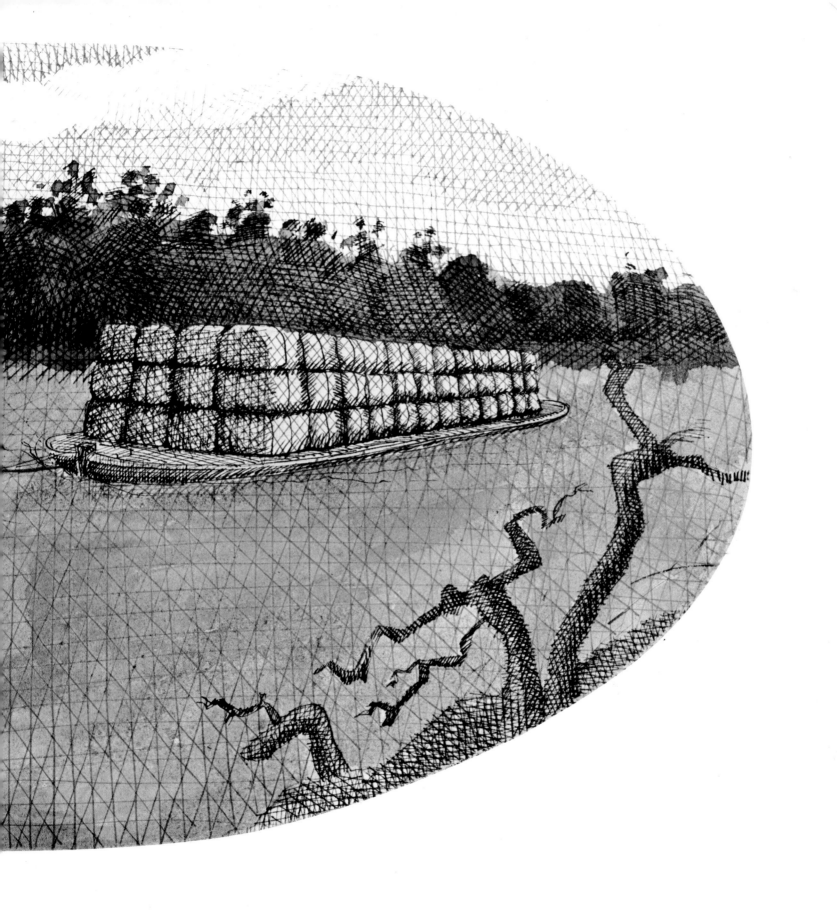

Captain Bill was the skipper.
He read the charts and maps
and steered the boat along the river.

Gus was the stoker.
He fired the boiler to keep the engines going
and the paddle-wheels turning.

Sam was the cook.
He prepared hearty meals for the riverboat crew.

At night the crew sat on the deck,
talking and telling stories . . .

One night, Captain Bill said,
'You know something?
I'd say I'm the most important man
on board this steamer'.
'Oh no you are not', said Gus, 'I am'.

Sam just smiled to himself.

Captain Bill and Gus argued and argued.
'Right', said Captain Bill at last,
'let's swap jobs.
Tomorrow you try steering
and I'll stoke the boiler'.
'O.K.', answered Gus,
'*then* we'll see who's most important'.

Sam still smiled and said nothing.

The next day they started off before breakfast.
Everything went well, until . . .

'This is hard work', puffed Captain Bill.
'I think I'll just sit down for a minute'.
While he rested, the fire went out
and the engine stopped.

'Crikey!' yelled Gus, 'I can't steer this boat —
I can't hold the wheel steady
and I don't know which way to go.
Oh, no! We're heading for the bank'.

Captain Bill came up on deck.
'Now you've done it', he shouted at Gus,
'you've snagged us on that fallen tree.
That wouldn't have happened if *I'd* been steering'.

'Well, why did the engine stop?' said Gus,
'*I* wouldn't have let the fire go out'.
They looked at each other glumly.
'Oh well, let's have a good hot breakfast
before we try to shift her', said Captain Bill.

'What's this, no breakfast?
Where's Sam then?
We can't possibly work on an empty stomach.'

They found Sam asleep in his bunk.
'Hey!' they shouted at him,
'Where's our breakfast?'
Sam opened one eye.
'Who's the most important man
on board this steamer?' he asked.
Captain Bill and Gus laughed.

'All right Sam, *you* are .'

So Sam got up and made breakfast.
Then they all sat down
and had hot pancakes and coffee,
and warm fresh bread.